Five Minutes' Peace

♫ "...with a little help from my friends." ♫

For Geoff, Sue, Abby, Hannah, Nick & Polly, with love.

First published 1986 by Walker Books Ltd
87 Vauxhall Walk, London SE11 5HJ

This edition published 1998

2 4 6 8 10 9 7 5 3 1

© 1986 Jill Murphy

Printed in Hong Kong

British Library Cataloguing in Publication Data
A catalogue record for this book is available
from the British Library.
ISBN 0-7445-5594-9 (Hbk)
ISBN 0-7445-6001-2 (Pbk)

Five Minutes' Peace

Jill Murphy

WALKER BOOKS
AND SUBSIDIARIES
LONDON • BOSTON • SYDNEY

The children were having breakfast.
This was not a pleasant sight.

Mrs Large took a tray from the cupboard.
She set it with a teapot, a milk jug, her
favourite cup and saucer, a plate of
marmalade toast and a leftover cake
from yesterday. She stuffed the morning
paper into her pocket and sneaked off
towards the door.

"Where are you going with that tray, Mum?" asked Laura.

"To the bathroom," said Mrs Large.

"Why?" asked the other two children.

"Because I want five minutes' peace from *you* lot," said Mrs Large.

"That's why."

"Can *we* come?" asked Lester as they trailed
   up the stairs behind her.

"No," said Mrs Large, "you can't."

"What shall *we* do then?" asked Laura.

"You can play," said Mrs Large. "Downstairs.
   By yourselves. And keep an eye on the baby."

"I'm *not* a baby," muttered the little one.

Mrs Large ran a deep, hot bath.
She emptied half a bottle of bath-foam into
the water, plonked on her bath-hat and got in.
She poured herself a cup of tea and lay back
with her eyes closed.
It was heaven.

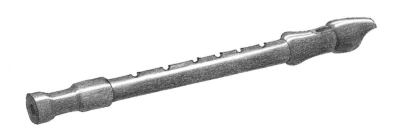

"Can I play you my tune?" asked Lester.

Mrs Large opened one eye. "Must you?" she asked.

"I've been practising," said Lester. "You told me to.
Can I? Please, just for *one* minute."

"Go *on* then," sighed Mrs Large.

So Lester played. He played "Twinkle, Twinkle,
Little Star" three and a half times.

In came Laura. "Can I read you a page from my reading book?" she asked.

"*No*, Laura," said Mrs Large. "Go on, *all* of you, off downstairs."

"You let Lester play his tune," said Laura.

"I heard. You like him better than me. It's not fair."

"Oh, don't be silly, Laura," said Mrs Large.

"Go *on* then. Just *one* page."

So Laura read. She read four and a half pages of "Little Red Riding Hood".

In came the little one with a trunkful of toys.
"For *you*!" he beamed, flinging them all
into the bath water.
"Thank you, dear," said Mrs Large weakly.

"Can I see the cartoons in the paper?" asked Laura.

"Can I have the cake?" asked Lester.

"Can I get in with you?" asked the little one.

Mrs Large groaned.

In the end they *all* got in. The
little one was in such a hurry that
he forgot to take off his pyjamas.

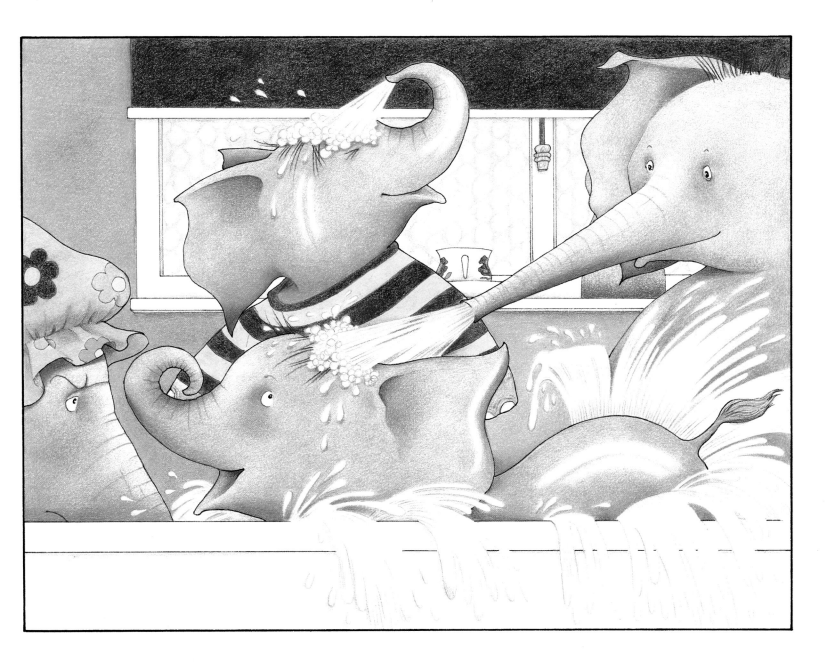

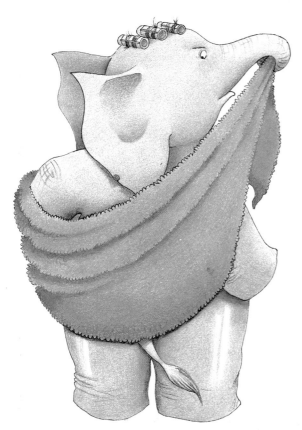

Mrs Large got out. She dried herself, put on her dressing-gown and headed for the door.

"Where are you going *now*, Mum?" asked Laura.

"To the kitchen," said Mrs Large.

"Why?" asked Lester.

"Because I want five minutes' peace from *you* lot," said Mrs Large.

"That's why."

And off she went downstairs, where she had three minutes and forty-five seconds of peace before they all came to join her.

MORE WALKER PAPERBACKS
For You to Enjoy

Some more Large Family books by Jill Murphy

ALL IN ONE PIECE

Highly Commended for the Kate Greenaway Medal

While Mr and Mrs Large get ready to go out for the evening,
Laura, Lester, Luke and the baby are busy making a mess!
ISBN 0-7445-6002-0   £4.99

A QUIET NIGHT IN

Shortlisted for the Kate Greenaway Medal

It's Mr Large's birthday and Mrs Large is planning a quiet night in –
without any children. But in the Large household things rarely go as planned!
"Delectably droll and rumbustious." *The Daily Mail*
ISBN 0-7445-6000-4   £4.99

A PIECE OF CAKE

Mrs Large puts the family on a diet of healthy food and exercise.
But when a cake arrives from Grandma, the family's resolve is sorely tested!
"The illustrations are pure delight… More rueful smiles from mothers everywhere." *The Lady*
ISBN 0-7445-6003-9   £4.99